W9-BAK-336

LUDLOW GROWS UP

© Copyright 1996 by Kelli C. Foster, Gina C. Erickson, and Kerri Gifford

All rights reserved.
No part of this book may be reproduced in any form,
by photostat, microfilm, xerography, or any other means,
or incorporated into any information retrieval system,
electronic or mechanical, without the written permission
of the copyright owner.

All inquiries should be addressed to:
Barron's Educational Series, Inc.
250 Wireless Boulevard
Hauppauge, NY 11788

International Standard Book Number 0-8120-9247-3

Library of Congress Catalog Card Number: 95-21027

Library of Congress Cataloging-in-Publication Data

Foster, Kelli C.
    Ludlow grows up / by Foster & Erickson ; illustrations by
Kerri Gifford.
        p. cm. — (Get ready—get set—read!)
    Summary: Ludlow the flower bulb is reluctant to grow up.
    ISBN 0-8120-9247-3
    (1. Bulbs (Botany)—Fiction. 2. Tulips—Fiction. 3. Stories in rhyme.)
I. Erickson, Gina Clegg. II. Gifford, Kerri, ill. III. Title. IV. Series: Erickson,
Gina Clegg. Get ready—get set—read!
PZ8.3.F813Lu   1996
(E)—dc20
                                                        95-21027
                                                            CIP
                                                            AC

PRINTED IN HONG KONG
6789 9927 9876543

GET READY...GET SET...READ!

LUDLOW GROWS UP

by
Foster & Erickson

Illustrations by
Kerri Gifford

BARRON'S

"There is no more snow.
It's time to grow."

"Let's each grow up
to make our row."

So up they went,
but not Ludlow.

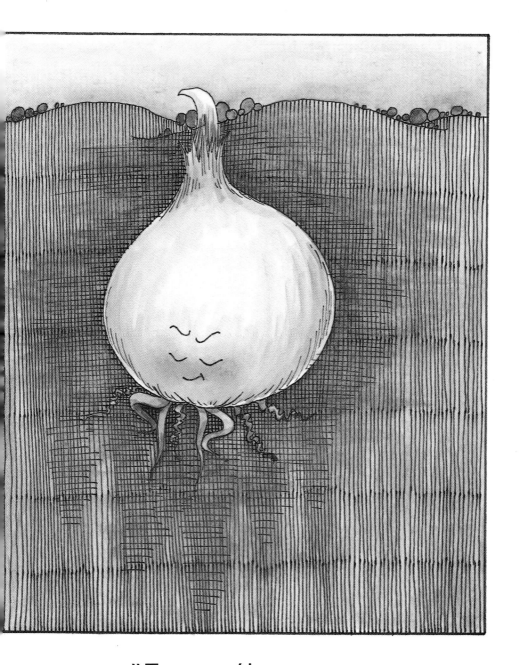

"I won't grow up.
I'll stay below!"

"Come on, Ludlow.
Don't be slow."

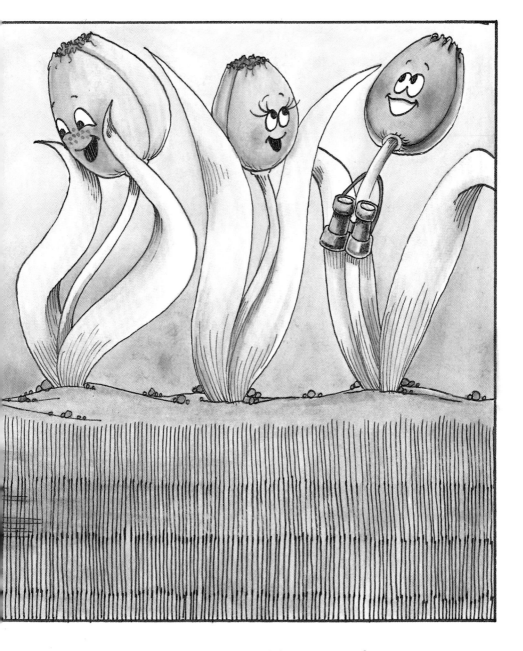

"It's so pretty up here,
you know."

"Oh no!
Up there the big winds blow."

"I like it here.
I'll stay below."

"The sun up here
will help you grow."

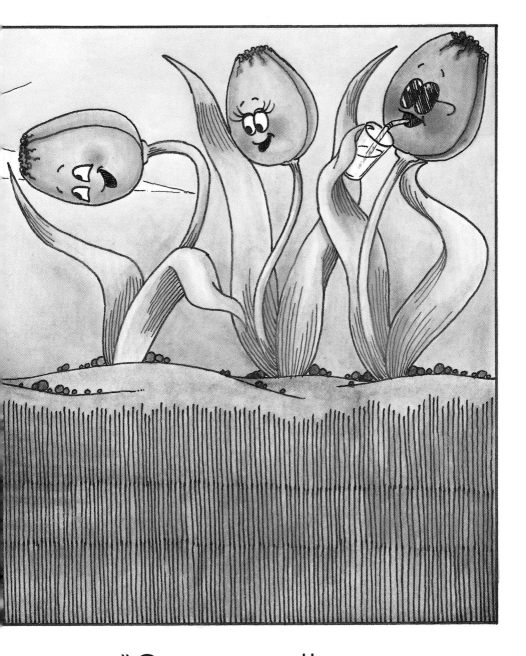

"Come see the sun.
Come see it glow."

"Oh no!
Up there the water flows."

"We love the rain.
It brings rainbows."

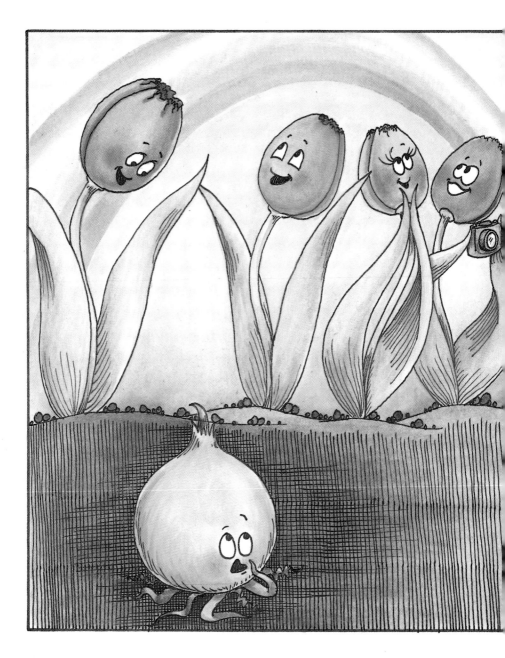

"Rainbows are red, yellow, green, purple, and blue."

"Show me the rainbow and
I'll grow up with you."

"With you, Ludlow,
we're a rainbow too!"

The End

The OW Word Family

blow
below
flows
glow
grow
know
Ludlow
rainbow
rainbows
row
show
snow

Sight Words

our
blue
don't
love
rain
they
stay
won't
green
water
pretty
purple
yellow

Dear Parents and Educators:

Welcome to *Get Ready...Get Set...Read!*

We've created these books to introduce children to the magic of reading.

Each story in the series is built around one or two word families. For example, *A Mop for Pop* uses the OP word family. Letters and letter blends are added to OP to form words such as TOP, LOP, and STOP. As you can see, once children are able to read OP, it is a simple task for them to read the entire word family. In addition to word families, we have used a limited number of "sight words." These are words found to occur with high frequency in the books your child will soon be reading. Being able to identify sight words greatly increases reading skill.

You might find the steps outlined on the facing page useful in guiding your work with your beginning reader.

We had great fun creating these books, and great pleasure sharing them with our children. We hope *Get Ready...Get Set...Read!* helps make this first step in reading fun for you and your new reader.

Kelli C. Foster, Ph.D.
Educational Psychologist

Gina Clegg Erickson, MA
Reading Specialist

Guidelines for Using *Get Ready...Get Set...Read!*

Step 1.   Read the story to your child.

Step 2.   Have your child read the Word Family list
           aloud several times.

Step 3.   Invent new words for the list. Print each new
           combination for your child to read.
           Remember, nonsense words can be used
           (*dat, kat, gat*).

Step 4.   Read the story *with* your child. He or she reads
           all of the Word Family words; you read the rest.

Step 5.   Have your child read the Sight Word list
           aloud several times.

Step 6.   Read the story *with* your child again. This time
           he or she reads the words from both lists;
           you read the rest.

Step 7.   Your child reads the entire book to you!

There are five sets of books in the

Series. Each set consists of five **FIRST BOOKS**
and two **BRING-IT-ALL-TOGETHER BOOKS**.

SET 1

is the first set your children should read.
The word families are selected from the short vowel sounds:
at, **ed**, **ish** and **im**, **op**, **ug**.

SET 2

provides more practice
with short vowel sounds:
an and **and**, **et**, **ip**, **og**, **ub**.

SET 3

focuses on
long vowel sounds:
ake, **eep**, **ide** and **ine**, **oke** and **ose**, **ue** and **ute**.

SET 4

introduces the idea that the word family sounds
can be spelled two different ways:
ale/ail, **een/ean**, **ight/ite**, **ote/oat**, **oon/une**.

SET 5

acquaints children with word families that
do not follow the rules for long and short vowel sounds:
all, **ound**, **y**, **ow**, **ew**.